THE CATNAPPING CAPER

Elizabeth Bryan Mysteries

Vicki Berger Erwin

To Ellen, Tammy, Sandy, Ann, Jill, Maureen, Sue,
Pat, Bev, and in absentia, Nancy, with love.
Thanks for all the time you've spent helping me
with my writing and being my friends.

Thanks to Dawn and Ruth for your friendship,
support, and your red pens!

Elizabeth Bryan Mysteries
The Disappearing Card Trick
The Case of the Questionable Cousin
The Catnapping Caper

Cover illustration by Sally Schaedler

Copyright © 1996 Concordia Publishing House
3558 S. Jefferson Avenue, St. Louis, MO 63118-3968
Manufactured in the United States of America

Library of Congress Cataloging-in-Publication Data

Erwin, Vicki Berger, 1951–
    The catnapping caper/Vicki Berger Erwin.
        p.   cm.   —(Elizabeth Bryan mysteries)
    Summary: When 12-year-old Elizabeth sets out to find a prize-winning
cat which disappears from a used bookstore, she encounters a mystery
involving rare books, secret messages, and a mysterious stranger.
    ISBN 0-570-04870-2
    [1. Cats—Fiction. 2. Mystery and detective stories. 3. Christian life—
Fiction.] I. Title. II. Series.
PZ7.E7445Cat 1996
[Fic]—dc20   96-33840

1 2 3 4 5 6 7 8 9 10   05 04 03 02 01 00 99 98 97 96

CONTENTS

1

EXIT (ALMOST) FINOLA

"This is the last place, I promise," Elizabeth said, holding the door handle to the Read It Again bookstore.

Justin remained firmly planted on the sidewalk in front of the store. "They said at the last place that you can't get the book. They said you can't even order it," he reminded Elizabeth.

"This is a *used* bookstore. It's the only place you can buy books that aren't published anymore. That's why I need to look here."

A young man burst out of the shop, pushing Elizabeth out of the way. She stumbled backward and would have fallen if she hadn't been holding the door. A woman followed, shaking her finger at the man. "Good riddance to bad rubbish, Gregory."

"The door!" the woman yelled. "Please shut

… Finola, come back here. Stop that cat!"

Elizabeth felt a tickling around her ankles and looked down. She reached for the gray ball of fur moving toward the street, but it slipped between her hands.

The man bent toward the cat, then straightened, stuck his hands in his jeans pockets, and stalked away.

Justin moved quickly and scooped up the cat. It yowled in protest, squirming and wriggling every which way. Stepping inside the bookstore, Justin dumped the cat on the floor.

Elizabeth barely had time to step inside and pull the door shut behind her to block the cat's second try at escape. It looked up at Elizabeth and meowed, then danced from paw to paw like it had some pressing business outside.

"Finola, bad kitty." The woman reached down and picked up the cat. It was so large, it hung all the way to the woman's knees. The cat looked at Elizabeth again, then at the door.

"That's the biggest cat I've ever seen," Justin said.

Elizabeth was so intrigued by the woman's hair that she barely noticed the size of the cat. Her hair, a strange orange-red color, stuck out in corkscrew curls from the woman's head like a mop. Elizabeth twisted a strand of her own red hair around her finger. She knew from experience how bad it was to have red hair, but orange would be even worse.

The woman cradled the cat like a baby and rocked it back and forth. "Thank you for capturing my runaway beauty. She's usually quite content to roam among her forest of books, but occasionally she takes it in her mind to breathe a bit of fresh air—don't you, pretty kitty?" The woman rubbed her cheek against the cat's head. She walked away, still holding the cat, and climbed a staircase on one side of the shop.

"I'll return shortly," the woman said when she was about halfway up. "Have a look about."

Elizabeth heard a door open overhead, then a crash. She started forward.

"It's okay," the woman yelled.

The next thing Elizabeth knew, a parade of cats came marching down the steps—an orange stripe, a black-and-gold calico, and a gray-and-white spotted. They were all smaller and sleeker than Finola, and they seemed to know exactly where they were going. The orange cat jumped into the display window and stared at the street.

The calico curled up on a table of children's books, and the gray-and-white cat disappeared down the row marked *Mystery*.

Elizabeth wandered around the small shop, trying to find the book she wanted. There were so many books everywhere—crammed into tall, dark wood shelves and stacked on the hardwood floors. She breathed in that special old-book smell of ink, yellowed paper, and a touch of mustiness. Elizabeth thought the cats were the perfect touch.

"She must like cats as much as you do," Justin said, trailing after her.

"Then she can't be all bad," said Elizabeth.

Stopping in the children's section, Elizabeth picked up a book and thumbed through it, then she picked up a second book. She dragged her hand along the spines of the books, twisting her head to read the sideways titles.

"Look, this is it. The series, I mean, that Mom's been collecting." She felt a huge sense of relief as she ran her finger across the row of dark blue bindings, searching for the title she needed.

Before he'd died, Elizabeth's dad had given her mother a volume from a series of favorite classics for children every year for her birthday.

Elizabeth had continued the tradition. This year she hadn't been able to find the books at any of the usual places. Finally, she'd remembered this used bookstore.

"*Heidi, Treasure Island, Tom Sawyer, Little Men, Little Women.* This is it, the one she needs." Elizabeth held up the copy of *Little Women.*

A phone rang, startling Elizabeth. It rang again and again.

"Get that, please!" the woman called from the top of the stairs.

Justin took a step toward the counter, then stopped and looked at Elizabeth. Reaching around Justin, she grabbed the receiver. "Hello," Elizabeth said.

"Is this Teresa?" a woman asked.

Elizabeth thought the elderly voice on the other end of the phone sounded familiar. "No," Elizabeth answered, figuring the woman with the cats must be Teresa.

"To whom *am* I speaking?" the woman asked.

"This is ..." The orange-haired woman jerked the phone out of Elizabeth's hand.

"Read It Again," the woman said into the receiver. "This is Teresa, Mrs. Baker. Yes, I'm sorry. I know you haven't received your books yet. Gregory was missing today, and I've had the sole responsibility of the shop ..."

She stopped speaking and leaned against the counter, her chin resting on her chest, her eyes closed. "By 5 P.M. ?" Pulling a tiny watch from the pocket of her denim jumper, Teresa sighed. "Yes, ma'am," she answered, then slowly replaced the phone.

"I do hope you will return some day and have a good, long browse through my garden of delights," said Teresa, "but I must rush you away for now. Duty calls as I have a delivery to deliver." She ran her fingers through the spiky orange hairdo, making it stick out even more.

Elizabeth opened the copy of *Little Women*, searching for a price. "I have just one question," she said. "I need this book for my mother's birthday ..."

"Tomorrow, tomorrow. I'll answer *all* your questions tomorrow." Teresa made shooing motions toward the door.

Elizabeth clutched the book she had been to every bookstore in town looking for. She wasn't going to let it get away now. Someone could come in and buy her book, her mom's book, before she got back. "The sign says you're open until six. It's only a little past four-thirty," Elizabeth said.

"Elizabeth, she wants us to leave," Justin whispered.

"I must get these books to Mrs. Baker within the half hour or I'll lose one of my best customers," Teresa said, a whine in her voice. "I'm most sorry. You saved my little Finola and this is how I repay you." She threw up her hands and looked at the ceiling.

"I only want to know how much this copy of *Little Women* costs." Elizabeth held up the blue-bound volume.

"Truly one of my favorite books!" Teresa said.

The bell on the door tinkled, signaling the arrival of another customer. "Mr. Smith! How wonderful to see you," Teresa said, her expression contradicting her words as her eyes widened. She clasped and unclasped her hands.

"Any chance I could have a look at that Hemingway you said was coming in? I'll browse while you get it," said Mr. Smith, a small man whose red cheeks and green sweater reminded Elizabeth of one of Santa's elves.

Teresa rubbed one hand back and forth over her lips. "Oh, dear, oh, dear," she said softly.

"What *is* it?" Elizabeth asked. The shop owner was becoming more agitated by the minute.

"Mr. Smith is also one of my best customers. And he looks in a buying mood. But if I don't deliver Mrs. Baker's parcel to her in …" Teresa looked at her watch again and her eyes got even bigger, "15 minutes, she'll never step foot in this shop again. Actually she hardly steps foot in here anyway, says the cats make her allergic. But she buys multitudes by phone.

"Curses, Gregory!" Teresa shook her fist. "Today of all days!"

"You wouldn't mean the Mrs. Baker who lives on Woodlawn, would you?" Elizabeth asked. No wonder the voice sounded familiar. Mrs. Baker attended her church, and Elizabeth knew from personal experience that the woman could be demanding. The day Elizabeth's youth group had raked her yard, Mrs. Baker had insisted they arrive by 11 A.M. or she'd never let them work for her again.

Justin gave Elizabeth a little poke in the middle of her back.

"You *know* Mrs. Baker?" Teresa asked. Elizabeth nodded. Justin poked her a little harder, and she swatted his hand away.

"Teresa, Teresa, what a fine selection!" Mr. Smith, his cheeks even rosier, dumped a stack of books on the counter. "And I've only begun." He disappeared between the shelves.

"Oh, my, oh, my." Teresa patted her lips nervously.

"I'll deliver the package for you if you'll hold this copy of *Little Women* for me until Monday afternoon," said Elizabeth.

"You'd *do* that? For me? But I don't *know* you. You could take these books, and I'd never see you or them again."

"My name is Elizabeth Bryan. I'm 12, and I go to North Middle School. I live on Brookhaven Court …" The orange striped cat wrapped itself around Elizabeth's legs, purring loudly.

"Why, look at that," said Teresa. "Duncan likes you. Why am I worried? Now that I think about it, Finola seemed to like you too, so you can't be all bad."

Teresa held up her hand. "I trust Duncan's judgment." She disappeared below the counter, then popped up, holding a stack of brown notebooks. "Gregory's notebooks," she said and looked at Elizabeth and Justin. "He left without his notebooks."

Elizabeth had no idea what she was talking about.

"An odd twist," Teresa murmured. She disappeared again.

When she came up, Teresa pressed a bag of books into Elizabeth's arms. "The *Little Women* is yours. Come by Monday and we'll do business. Boy, you come too. I'll serve tea, a tea fit for the prince and princess who rescued my precious cat and saved the day!"

The bell tinkled as Teresa opened the door and ushered them out. She waved through the window as Elizabeth and Justin walked past.

"Isn't she the most interesting woman?" Elizabeth said. "The way she talks!"

Justin rolled his eyes.

"I can't wait until our tea party," Elizabeth said as she trailed behind Justin, glancing back at the store. "How long do we have to get to Mrs. Baker's?"

"About seven minutes," Justin answered. They both walked a little faster.

"The store must belong to Teresa. Imagine

having your own bookstore," said Elizabeth.

"And look at the problems. That guy walked out, leaving her with a mess," Justin said.

"Gregory. Strange, huh? I wonder what's so important about those notebooks Teresa found," said Elizabeth.

"Why do you keep calling her 'Teresa'?"

"What else do I call her? Besides I don't know ... Oops, here, turn here," she said, almost passing Mrs. Baker's small house. It was tucked between two larger houses like a child standing between its parents.

"Mrs. Baker can be difficult," Elizabeth said to Justin. "This would be a good time to use your dimples."

"What do you mean?" Justin asked, turning red. Elizabeth grinned at him as she rang the doorbell.

Mrs. Baker peeked through the living-room curtains. Elizabeth heard her coming toward the door, her walker thumping with each step. Mrs. Baker opened the door a crack, the security chain still in place.

"Hi, Mrs. Baker. Remember me? Elizabeth Bryan, from church. I helped rake your lawn last fall."

"And I paid you fair and square then. You aren't getting another penny from me," Mrs. Baker said.

"No! No, that has nothing to do with why I'm here." Elizabeth held up the package and opened the storm door. "I'm delivering your books from Read It Again."

"My books?" Mrs. Baker unhooked the chain and opened the door wide enough for the books to pass through. "There's no cat hair on these, is there? All those cats set my allergies off like a rocket. Can't even go in the store anymore."

"No cat hair that I know of," said Elizabeth, although with a cat as fluffy as Finola, she wouldn't bet on it.

"You're not Gregory," Mrs. Baker said to Justin. "You have blond hair and you're wearing a hat. Gregory never wears a hat." Justin quickly removed his baseball cap and tried to make his hair lie flat.

"You working for that girl Teresa?" Mrs. Baker asked Elizabeth.

"Just doing her a favor," said Elizabeth. "Maybe I'll see you at church Sunday." She and Justin backed away from the door.

"Why didn't that Gregory bring me my books?" Mrs. Baker asked.

"I think maybe he quit," said Elizabeth.

"He quits once a week," said Mrs. Baker. "So peculiar, isn't it, the way he's always writing in those notebooks? But I'm anxious to find out what's going to happen in the next chapter of his book."

"His book?" asked Elizabeth. Gregory got more interesting with each bit of information she heard.

"He's writing a book about the murder," Mrs. Baker said in hushed tones.

"The murder?"

"The one that happened at the bookstore," said Mrs. Baker in a tone that let Elizabeth know the woman didn't think she was too bright.

"There was a murder in the bookstore? When?" Elizabeth shivered at the thought.

"Long before your time, missy. Long before Gregory's too. But he's obsessed with it. I'm helping him since I *was* around then and knew the man who was murdered."

"Who was it?" Elizabeth asked.

"Ask Gregory," said Mrs. Baker. "I'd stay away from that shop if I were you. It's not a happy place. Good things don't come out of there." Mrs. Baker slammed the door.

Justin shook his head. "Why'd she say that?"

Elizabeth smiled. A murder! She wondered if it had been solved and why Gregory was so interested in it. She couldn't wait to go back to Read It Again—or to find out more about the mysterious Gregory and his notebooks.

2

NO CAUSE FOR CELEBRATION

"Do we really have to do this tea party thing?" Justin asked. "Can't we pick up your book and go? I have newspapers to deliver, then some of the guys are shooting baskets at school."

"Teresa's expecting you too. After all, you're the one who actually caught Finola. Let her say thank you, then you can go," said Elizabeth.

"Elizabeth, Justin, wait up!" Turning and walking backwards, Elizabeth waited for her best friend, Meghan, to catch up.

"What have you been doing lately? It's like I only see you when you're on the way to do something else," Meghan said, hitching her backpack higher on her shoulder.

Justin and Elizabeth exchanged looks.

"I knew it! You're going someplace now." Meghan folded her arms across her chest and stuck out her lower lip.

"We're going to pick up my mom's birthday present," said Elizabeth.

"I'll come along," said Meghan. "You know how I love to shop. What are you going to get her? Clothes? Perfume?"

"A book," said Elizabeth, adding slowly, "and you can't exactly come along."

Meghan's thick eyebrows drew together, forming a dark line above her eyes.

"Saturday we, Justin really, rescued the bookstore owner's cat, and she's invited us to tea to thank us," Elizabeth explained. "But you have to come with me next time. You'll love this woman."

"You could take my place," Justin grumbled.

"I'll call you tonight and tell you about it," said Elizabeth.

"Promise?" asked Meghan.

Elizabeth held up two fingers. "On my honor!"

"Guess I might as well go home." Meghan turned and walked the other way, her shoulders sagging.

"I'll call you!" Elizabeth yelled.

Meghan waved but didn't turn around.

"She would probably love this tea thing," said Justin.

"She seems a little down," said Elizabeth, taking one more look at her friend. "I'll call her tonight and see what's going on."

The bell rang as they opened the door to the store. Elizabeth and Justin waited for Teresa to appear. "Hello?" said Elizabeth. She walked to the counter, then to the foot of the staircase. "Hello?" she called a little louder.

"Maybe she's in the bathroom," said Justin. He picked up a book with football players on the cover and started looking through it.

"The door's unlocked, so she couldn't be too far away," Elizabeth said.

She walked down the mystery row, identified on the end of the shelf by a magnifying glass. Elizabeth sat down beside a stack of books and pulled out an Agatha Christie she wasn't sure she'd read. The next thing she knew, the black-and-gold calico cat had settled itself in her lap.

"Justin, look, one of the cats," said Elizabeth, running her hand down the cat's sleek back.

"I have one too," said Justin, joining her with the orange striped cat hanging around his neck. "It's even friendlier than your Tiger."

"I guess they have to be pretty laid back to deal with all the customers," said Elizabeth. "Can you imagine Dolores with so many people around?"

"What customers? It's us. And where's Teresa? Let's go, Elizabeth." Justin put the cat on the floor. It rubbed against his legs, purring loudly.

"I have to get that book," she reminded him.

A door opened at the back of the store and Teresa entered, looking intently around the store. Her eyes landed on Elizabeth and Justin. Elizabeth felt like Teresa was looking right through her.

"Did you see her?" Teresa asked. "Finola. Did you see Finola anyplace outside—or in here?"

Elizabeth and Justin shook their heads in unison.

"She's vanished, escaped, or … . And with kittens due to arrive momentarily. What am I going to do? *What* am I going to do?" Teresa approached Elizabeth and took her arm, staring into the young girl's eyes as she spoke.

Elizabeth backed away. "You could put up

signs or call the animal shelter. If she doesn't return soon, you could run an ad in the paper."

"Yes, yes. If she simply walked out the door that perhaps would work," Teresa said, nodding vigorously.

"What do you mean, *if* she walked out?" Justin asked.

"Ha, ha, ha," Teresa laughed unconvincingly. "Nothing, nothing at all. Of course she escaped."

The bell tinkled. Everyone looked to see who was coming into the store.

"Amy Catherine!" Elizabeth said, surprised to see one of her classmates.

"Hi," Amy Catherine said, turning a bright pink, as if embarrassed to be seen in the bookstore.

"You know one another?" Teresa asked. "Amy is truly one of my extraordinary customers. And may I inquire what you are seeking today?"

Elizabeth was amazed at how Teresa could be a wreck about her cat one minute and the next minute deal with a customer like nothing was wrong.

"Just looking," Amy Catherine mumbled. She reached up and grabbed a book from a top shelf, then folded herself into a chair at the end of the row.

"And I'm here to buy that copy of *Little Women*. You said you'd hold it," Elizabeth said.

"Yes, indeed. *Little Women*, Brandywine Illustrated Classic, 1965, a first edition in mint condition," Teresa said as she moved toward the counter. "A bargain at $125."

Elizabeth gasped. "A hundred and twenty-five dollars! I bought *Heidi* last year for $18."

"Ah! But not a first edition, *and* the books were still in print." Teresa laid the book on the counter. "Oh, I failed to account for the fee I owe you for safe and prompt delivery of Mrs. Baker's books. That amounts to a deduction of $5."

Tears burned Elizabeth's eyes. It was a tradition to get Mom one of the classics for her birthday. But $125—where would she get that kind of money?

"Don't you have one of the cheaper ones?" Elizabeth asked, her voice sounding ragged as she tried not to cry.

"I have a set," Amy Catherine said.

"I'll buy *Little Women*," Elizabeth offered quickly.

"I don't think my mom would let me," Amy Catherine said, "but I could ask."

"That's okay," said Elizabeth. Amy Catherine's mom would never let her break up a set of books. In fact, Elizabeth was surprised Amy Catherine's mom let her buy used books.

"Perhaps we could create an arrangement," Teresa said. "I am in dire need of a young, energetic assistant to deliver orders to certain of my clientele unable to brave the great out-of-doors for whatever reason. Five dollars a delivery …"

"I'll do it," Elizabeth said.

"Another five if you'll be so kind as to post announcements of Finola's disappearance," Teresa added.

"We'll do that anyway," said Elizabeth, automatically including Justin in the agreement. "I know how I'd feel if one of my cats was lost." In fact, the thought made her feel so awful she could hardly bear it.

"I'll help too," Amy Catherine offered. "Which one is Finola?"

"The *huge* one," said Justin.

"She's going to have babies," Elizabeth and Teresa said at the same time. They laughed.

"And what would be your procedure if your cat was catnapped?" Teresa asked, pursing her lips.

"Catnapped? Do you think …" Elizabeth felt a tingling along her spine. Mrs. Baker was right. There was something different about this store. And after solving two mysteries, Elizabeth was always on the lookout for another.

"Mercy me, no. Just a supposition," Teresa said. "I like to see how creative and imaginative my employees can be." She laughed another *ha, ha, ha.*

"You don't have to worry about that with Elizabeth," Justin said in a low voice. Elizabeth gave him a dirty look.

"So we have a deal? I'll save the book, and you'll be in my employ?" asked Teresa. Elizabeth nodded.

"Magnificent. I'll retire to my desk to begin creating a Missing Cat Flyer," Teresa announced. "Why don't you begin acquainting yourself with your new office."

Elizabeth barely heard her new boss. She was too busy savoring the thought of her first real job besides baby-sitting. And maybe there'd even be another mystery to solve. Despite Teresa's assurance, Elizabeth couldn't erase the possibility that Finola hadn't gotten out on her own. What if she *had* been catnapped?

3

MISSING CATS

Amy Catherine led Elizabeth on a tour of the store, stopping at all her favorite books, while Teresa printed, then copied, a LOST flyer for Finola.

"I didn't know you liked to read," Elizabeth said to Amy Catherine. "Sometimes I feel like I'm the only one in school who ever reads anything except what we have to."

"Hey, I read," said Justin.

"*Sports Illustrated* and *Sporting News* don't count," Elizabeth said.

"As my mom says, 'At least he's reading,'" Justin said with a grin.

"That's one of the reasons I come here," said Amy Catherine. "I read so much my mom hates to pay full price. You'll have to come over sometime and see my library."

"I'd love to," Elizabeth answered. The last

time Amy Catherine had invited her over was the night of the science fair, and Elizabeth had been tied up—literally—solving a mystery.

"Here you go. This should be enough to plaster the community and announce Finola's disappearance," said Teresa, handing each one of them a thick sheaf of papers.

Elizabeth looked at the flyer. The picture of Finola in the center of the page gave no clue to how big she really was. "MISSING CATS" was printed across the top. "Mother Finola and her unborn kittens lost" spread across the page under the picture. At the very bottom were the details: "Gray, long-hair, VERY expectant. Call 555-0290. Reward: Pick of the litter."

"Not everyone will be anxious to collect that reward," Justin whispered to Elizabeth. Teresa handed them masking tape and thumbtacks.

"I'll take Kirkwood Road to my house and put them up at the grocery store, library, and Farmer's Market," said Amy Catherine.

"I'll take the other side of Kirkwood Road," said Elizabeth.

"And I'll go up to Manchester," said Justin.

"I'll visit all the shops lining the main thoroughfare when my day here ends," said Teresa, "Or sooner if Gregory would happen back." She looked out the window as if she expected to see him appear.

"Do you have any books you want me to deliver along the way?" Elizabeth asked, anxious to start her new job.

"Not today. Tomorrow perhaps," said Teresa.

"Guess I'll see you then," Elizabeth said to her new boss.

"Right-o," Teresa answered, still looking out the window. "I do feel so much better thinking that someone might soon report a sighting to me."

"Elizabeth, I'll try to remember to bring that book, *Man Who Loved Clowns*, to school tomorrow. You'll love it," said Amy Catherine.

Justin, Elizabeth, and Amy Catherine scattered in three directions. Elizabeth stopped to attach signs to every pole and trash can that she passed. When she turned the corner and saw the dance studio where she took classes twice a week, Elizabeth groaned and turned back toward Read It Again.

Teresa was *still* staring out the window as

Elizabeth approached the store. Teresa started when Elizabeth opened the door. "I thought you were ... someone else," she said. Elizabeth noticed she was holding the brown notebooks—Gregory's notebooks.

"I can't come tomorrow," Elizabeth said. "I have a dance class after school. Usually it's in the evening, but we're having a special session with a guest instructor. I'll stay longer the day after."

Teresa forced a smile. "That's acceptable."

Elizabeth stepped outside, then walked inside once more. "What do I call you?" she asked.

"Teresa, of course. That's my name."

"Not Ms. ...?"

The bookstore owner shook her head, making her orange-red mop quiver all the way to the roots. "Teresa. I insist."

Why was it that, all of a sudden, adults were insisting that Elizabeth call them by their first name? First Mr. Hamilton, now Teresa. Elizabeth thought she probably knew why Mr. Hamilton, Don, as he wanted to be called, was pushing her to use his first name. Mr. Hamilton was her Mom's friend, the only man Mom had gone out with more than once or twice since Dad died. In fact, Elizabeth had lost track of how many times they'd gone out. One "date" almost ran into another, he was at their house so much. Her brother, Mike, was crazy about the man, and Mom obviously liked him. Elizabeth wasn't so sure. She knew she wasn't ready to call him Don.

The phone rang, and Teresa dove for it. "Gregory! Where are you?" Teresa turned her back to Elizabeth.

Although Teresa spoke in almost a whisper, Elizabeth thought she heard the woman ask, "What have you done with Finola?"

Turning back to Elizabeth, her face stripped of color, Teresa waved. "Thank you so much for your assistance. I'll look forward to your return." She held the phone against her chest and waved again.

Elizabeth backed out the door, watching as Teresa talked furiously into the phone, then slammed the receiver down and covered her face with her hands.

Reading the missing cat flyer again, Elizabeth wondered why it was so important for them to post the signs if Teresa already suspected what had happened to Finola.

4

A Prayer
for Finola

Even after tacking and taping flyers all along the route home, Elizabeth had some left. She decided she'd take them to school with her. Kids came from all over town to North Middle School, and someone might have seen Finola.

Elizabeth slowed her pace when she saw Mr. Hamilton's car parked in the driveway. If she wanted to tell Mom about her new job and the missing cat, she'd have to tell *him* too. She just wasn't ready to have Don Hamilton stopping by so often. And besides, Mr. Hamilton wouldn't understand. He hated cats.

"Mom, I'm home!" Elizabeth called out as she dropped her backpack by the stairs.

"We're in the kitchen. Why are you so late?" Mom came into the hallway holding a head of lettuce and trailing water across the floor.

"I got a job," Elizabeth said.

"A job?" Mom's mouth dropped open.

"Delivering books for Read It Again bookstore."

"I like that place," Mr. Hamilton said as he joined Mom and Elizabeth, took the lettuce from Mom, and carried it back to the sink.

"How did that come about?" Aunt Nan asked, continuing to stir what smelled like spaghetti sauce.

"Oh, hi, Aunt Nan," said Elizabeth. The older woman wasn't really related to the Bryans, but she'd lived next door since Elizabeth was a baby. Elizabeth and her brother had grown up calling her *Aunt*.

"So tell us," said Mom.

"I was in there looking around, and Teresa, the woman who owns the store, needed a package of books delivered to Mrs. Baker, you know, from our church …"

"Dottie Baker? That poor woman. What a sad, sad life she's had. Outlived two husbands and three children. She's a lonely soul," said Aunt Nan. "We need to remember her in our prayers."

"I delivered the books, and Teresa said I

could do more to help out around the store. Isn't that great?" said Elizabeth.

"Terrific," Mom said, giving Elizabeth a hug.

"Do you get a discount?" Mr. Hamilton asked.

"I didn't ask," said Elizabeth. She handed the lost cat flyer to Mom. "And Teresa lost her cat, a pregnant cat. We put these up on the way home—Justin and Amy Catherine and me. I thought I'd take some to school tomorrow."

Mr. Hamilton read the paper over Mom's shoulder. Just as Elizabeth expected, he said, "Finola? What kind of name is that for a cat? And the reward is pick of the litter? Great, let's go out and look right now. You guys need a few more cats."

Mom frowned at Mr. Hamilton.

"The cat looks like a Finola. Just like Dolores looks like a Dolores," Elizabeth said as pleasantly as she could.

"Tiger *does* look like his name," Mr. Hamilton said, pointing to the orange striped cat searching the floor for crumbs.

"You've had an exciting day, and you're probably hungry," Mom said. "Dinner will be ready in a little while. Mike is upstairs supposedly reading for his book report ..."

"That reminds me. Amy Catherine is going to lend me that book by the author who visited our school. She and I like a lot of the same books," said Elizabeth.

"Amy Catherine reads almost as much as you do. I had her in class last year," said Mom. She was a teacher at North Middle School. "Could you set the table for me? Don and Aunt Nan are both eating with us. Thanks, sweetie."

Elizabeth started getting the dishes down from the cabinet. She paused with a stack of plates in her hands. "Mom, do you think it's okay to ask God to watch over Finola and get her home safely?" Elizabeth asked. She'd wondered about praying for the cat all the way home.

"God created cats just the same as He created everything else," said Aunt Nan. "You go ahead and say that prayer." Aunt Nan never let a chance go by to encourage Elizabeth's reliance on God and His love for her and her family.

"Hey, Elizabeth," Mr. Hamilton said, "if you have extra flyers, I'll take a couple and post them at the high school."

The offer caught Elizabeth off guard, and she realized she was smiling at the enemy as she handed him a stack of signs.

 5

MESSAGE IN THE BOOKS

Amy Catherine was waiting at Elizabeth's locker after school the next day. "I've been trying to catch up with you all day," she said as Elizabeth and Meghan walked up. "Here's the book."

"Thanks." Elizabeth stuck it in her backpack along with her math and science books.

"I can't believe we have so much homework and a dance class tonight," Meghan complained as she opened the locker next to Elizabeth's. She dropped her bulging backpack on the floor. She pulled a rubber band out of her jeans pocket and wrapped it around her long brown hair.

"Are you working today?" Amy Catherine asked Elizabeth. "I wonder if Finola has turned up yet."

Elizabeth shook her head. "Meghan and I have a special dance class this afternoon."

Meghan walked through a step, then asked, "Work where, and who's Finola?"

"Elizabeth has a job at a bookstore," Amy Catherine answered before Elizabeth could get a word out. "Finola is the owner's cat. We put up flyers all over town yesterday afternoon."

"I thought you were shopping for your Mom's birthday present," Meghan said. The corners of her mouth turned down slightly, clueing Elizabeth that her friend was upset.

"I *was* shopping—at the bookstore. Amy Catherine shops there too," Elizabeth explained.

Meghan nodded but said nothing. She leaned down and picked up her backpack.

"We need to get going," Elizabeth said to Meghan. "Thanks, for the book, Amy Catherine. I'll get it back to you as soon as I finish."

"Take your time," said Amy Catherine. "I'll probably see you at Read It Again." She waved as Elizabeth and Meghan hurried away.

"A new job? Is that why you didn't have time to call me last night like you promised?" Meghan asked.

"I got home late, and I had tons of homework," said Elizabeth. "I thought I'd tell you at lunch, but I didn't see you."

Meghan groaned. "I have science just before lunch, and we were doing that experiment. My lab partner was Jenny Cohen. You know what a ditz she is. Our experiment fell apart about halfway through, and we had to start all over. I ate my sandwich in the lab so we could finish. Now I'm starving. Could we stop for a snack?"

"You and your snacks!" Elizabeth said. She looked at her watch and made a quick calculation. If they walked fast and Meghan got a cookie at the bakery, she might have time to check with Teresa about Finola.

"You're right. I could probably lose weight if I didn't eat and did this extra dance class," Meghan said.

"You don't need to lose weight," Elizabeth said. Meghan was short and always concerned about getting fat when she had no reason at all to worry. "You get a cookie at the bakery while I go see if the cat is back. But we have to hurry!"

Meghan ducked into the bakery, and Elizabeth ran a few doors down to Read It Again.

"Hello, Teresa?" Elizabeth called as she opened the door. Just like the day before, the shop seemed deserted. Elizabeth didn't see even one cat.

"I'm up here." Teresa stood at the top of the steps, eyes red, twisting a tissue between her hands.

"What's wrong?"

Teresa burst into hiccuping sobs—*hic, hic, wail, hic, hic, wail*. Elizabeth ran up the stairs, then stood staring at Teresa, not sure what to do. She looked around, searching for a kitchen or a bathroom. Maybe she could get her a glass of water.

The upstairs was as cluttered as the shop but not with books. Elizabeth had never seen so many awards and trophies. The walls were covered with prize ribbons—red, blue, white, and purple. Trophies lined shelves built along the wall, and there were pictures of Teresa and Finola everywhere.

No wonder Teresa was so upset, thought Elizabeth as she read a framed clipping that praised Finola. The cat wasn't just a pet, she was a *champion!* "All these ribbons?"

"Finola's," Teresa managed to say before she burst into sobs again.

"Has something happened to Finola?" Elizabeth asked, fearing the worst. What else could make Teresa so upset?

Teresa shook her head. She gulped and wiped her eyes. "Now Duncan is gone too. And the notebooks. Gregory's notebooks!"

Another cat gone? And the notebooks? Elizabeth glanced at the front door. There was more going on here than careless customers letting cats out, especially if there were other things missing.

"I'm keeping Shelley and Keats up here," Teresa said. "I'm too frightened to let them out of my sight."

"Have you called anyone? the police?" asked Elizabeth.

"The police!" Teresa looked like Elizabeth had suggested calling an exterminator. "No, not the police. We shan't call the authorities."

"But Teresa, losing two cats in two days. And other things …"

"I must be more vigilant," Teresa said, waving her wet tissue around.

"Does Gregory know his notebooks are gone?" Elizabeth asked.

"Gregory!" Teresa's voice rose an octave. "Even the sound of his name thrusts a knife into my heart." She patted her chest. "He does not know, and he will not know, unless he comes to his senses and returns home."

"Maybe you should call the police about Gregory," said Elizabeth.

Teresa shook her head. The bell tinkled and Mr. Smith, the elf-man Elizabeth had seen in the shop the first day, entered.

Teresa wiped her eyes and dabbed at her nose. "I know you must think I'm awful, not closing the store and devoting all my time to seeking Finola and Duncan. But if I neglect my business, my poor babies won't have a home to come back to. I thank you for your concern about my felines. But go on home. I feel certain Finola and Duncan will soon return to their humble abode safe and sound."

Poor Teresa. Elizabeth knew she'd rather be looking for the cats. At least Elizabeth knew she'd feel that way if it was her cats. If Teresa couldn't look, Elizabeth decided she'd do everything she could to help her.

Mr. Smith stood at a table Elizabeth had never noticed before. There were only two books displayed there, both standing upright. One was a small pink paperback with the title *I Surrender*. The second was a hardcover with a black-and-white dust cover, the title—*Tell Me What You Want*.

"Those books *aren't* available for purchase," Teresa said, louder than necessary.

Mr. Smith knocked the black-and-white book flat as he jerked in surprise. Teresa quickly replaced the book, looking over her shoulder toward the window.

That's when Elizabeth realized that the table was perfectly located to attract the attention of passersby. Why was Teresa wasting it on those two books?

Meghan was standing outside, her face pressed against the window. Teresa knocked on the glass and motioned for her to move.

"That's my friend, Meghan. She's waiting for me," said Elizabeth.

"She's blocking the window," said Teresa.

Elizabeth looked at the display again. It wasn't likely to draw too many people. *I Surrender. Tell Me What You Want.* Elizabeth repeated the titles a few times. Together they sounded like a message. Was Teresa trying to tell someone something?

"Thank you for stopping by, dear, you've been a great comfort. I'll see you tomorrow," said Teresa.

When Elizabeth walked out of the bookstore, she looked at the people passing by. No one even slowed down to look in the window.

"We're going to be late, and Miss Karen isn't going to like it," Meghan warned.

"Teresa is missing another cat," said Elizabeth.

"Are you going to put up more signs?"

"That's something I could do. Or maybe add Duncan's name to the ones already up," said Elizabeth.

"Where did you put them?" asked Meghan.

"Everywhere," said Elizabeth. "Just look ..." She pointed at a pole and realized only the tack and a tiny scrap of paper caught underneath it remained. She checked every pole and trash can on the way to the dance studio. She didn't see one flyer.

6

REASONS
FOR SUSPICION

"That was a terrific class yesterday," Elizabeth said to Meghan as they walked out of school and down the street.

"You think that because you caught on right away," said Meghan. "I thought it was kind of hard."

"Can you walk part of the way with me? I have to go to work," said Elizabeth.

"I was hoping you could help me a little with some of the new steps," said Meghan. "I know Miss Karen will want us to go through the whole thing again next Tuesday."

Elizabeth shook her head. "I wish I could. Maybe tomorrow if there's nothing for me to do at the store."

Meghan sighed.

"Hey, Elizabeth, Meghan, wait up!"

"Oh, no, it's Amy Catherine," Meghan said. "Keep walking and pretend you didn't hear."

"I can't do that," said Elizabeth. She stopped.

"Did you get a chance to read that book?" Amy Catherine asked.

"Some of it. It's good," said Elizabeth. "I'm going to try to finish it tonight."

Meghan stood to one side. Elizabeth motioned for her to come closer, but Meghan looked away with a bored expression on her face.

"I have to get to work," Elizabeth said to Amy Catherine.

"I might stop by later," said Amy Catherine. "Okay?"

Elizabeth shrugged and looked at Meghan again. She was intently studying her hair for split ends.

"Bye," said Amy Catherine as she ran to the van waiting at the curb. As soon as she got inside, Amy Catherine leaned out the window. "Do you want a ride?" she asked.

"No thanks," Elizabeth said, joining Meghan. "Bye."

"So you have time to read Amy Catherine's book?" asked Meghan.

"I read every night before I go to sleep," explained Elizabeth, feeling a little hurt by Meghan's unspoken accusation. "Anyway, I want to talk to you about Teresa's missing cats. I think they were catnapped."

Meghan looked surprised.

"Let me tell you why," said Elizabeth. She felt an arm around her neck and stopped. "What …?"

"Hi, Sherlock. Hi, Meghan," said Justin. "I heard what you just said."

"Then listen to why I said it." Elizabeth shrugged his arm from across her shoulders.

"I'm listening," said Justin.

"First, I heard Teresa on the phone asking Gregory—probably the same Gregory that almost knocked me down that first day—what he'd done with Finola." She ticked the point off on one finger, then held up two fingers. "Second, another cat is missing. And third, do you see any of the flyers we put up? I know I personally put up about 20. Somebody came along and tore them all down."

Elizabeth paused for effect and then continued. "Fourth, Teresa said Gregory was missing too, but she won't call the police. Then she got very upset when Mr. Smith touched a weird book display. She also didn't want Meghan blocking the window."

"What kind of display? I didn't notice anything," said Meghan. They'd reached the corner where Meghan turned to go home.

"That's why it's so weird," Elizabeth said. "It was kind of a nondisplay. The table was right in front of the window, but it only had two books on it. The title of one was *I Surrender* and the other was *Tell Me What You Want*."

"They don't sound like books I'd read, but they aren't that weird," said Justin.

"But you can see the table from the window *and* Teresa said they weren't for sale. When one fell over, she fixed it right away," Elizabeth explained. "Listen. *I surrender. Tell me what you want.*"

"So?" said Meghan.

"Don't you get it? They're a message," said Elizabeth, "to the catnapper. Teresa gives up and is willing to give him whatever he wants."

"Kind of a jump, isn't it?" asked Meghan.

Elizabeth was used to everyone doubting her suspicions, but it didn't keep her from getting irritated with her friends when it happened. "You just don't get it," she said.

"But Amy Catherine probably does,"

Meghan shot back. "Tell *her* this fantasy." She turned the corner and stomped off toward home.

"Meghan," Elizabeth called to her friend's back.

"Call me later. *If* you can tear yourself away from your reading," Meghan said.

"What was that all about?" Justin asked.

Elizabeth's feelings were at war. She couldn't decide if she was mad at Meghan for acting so silly about Amy Catherine or if she was hurt because her best friend since nursery school seemed mad at her and didn't take her seriously. She watched until Meghan disappeared.

"Elizabeth, did you two have a fight?" Justin asked.

"Not really. Meghan doesn't like Amy Catherine and I do. She doesn't like it that I've seen Amy Catherine a couple times at the bookstore. I don't understand."

"Don't ask me to explain," said Justin. "Girls' minds are pretty much beyond me."

"I'll call Meghan later and try to talk to her, but right now I've got to get to work," said Elizabeth.

"Maybe Finola and the other cat will be

back," said Justin.

"Maybe. Where are you going?"

"I think I'll come along and see this mysterious display. Maybe I can figure out today's secret message," Justin said and smiled.

"Stop teasing. I'm serious. Something strange is happening at the store. That place can be pretty creepy."

"Maybe you should quit your job," suggested Justin.

"I can't. I have to get that book for my mother."

"Maybe Teresa is holding Gregory's notebooks hostage, and he took the cats to get the notebooks back," said Justin.

"Nope. The notebooks are missing too," said Elizabeth. They stopped at the window and Elizabeth pointed at the table, then dropped her hand. The table was bare.

"Nice table," said Justin.

"If you'd seen the books *and* how Teresa acted ..." Elizabeth began. As they looked through the window, Teresa appeared, carrying an armload of books. When she saw them, she frowned, then dumped the books on the bare table and came to the door.

"Are you coming in?" Teresa asked.

"I'm ready to work," said Elizabeth, feeling like she'd been caught doing something she shouldn't. Yet she didn't have any idea what that something was.

"Has Finola shown up yet?" Justin asked. "I noticed all the signs were down."

"Or Duncan? or Gregory?" Elizabeth added.

Teresa gave her a strange look, then shook her head. "And she, poised on the brink of motherhood." There was a tiny catch in her voice.

"Her kittens are due," Elizabeth whispered to Justin.

"I've scheduled three deliveries for this afternoon, all in close geographic proximity," Teresa said to Elizabeth.

"I think she means books, not kittens," murmured Justin.

Elizabeth elbowed him to keep quiet. "Great." She added it up and mentally credited $15 toward her mother's birthday present.

"I've created an itinerary for the deliveries," Teresa continued, "arranging them from addresses closest to the shop to those most distant.

Please feel free to rearrange according to your preference."

Elizabeth nodded. "I've got to go," Justin said. "See you tomorrow."

Both Elizabeth and Teresa waved as he passed the window. "This is a great view of everybody passing by," Elizabeth said.

"When there is time to people-watch," Teresa said.

"Where are Shelley and Keats?" Elizabeth asked.

"Safe," said Teresa. "Now, I have the books packaged and the address of each buyer posted on the outside of the wrapping."

"Has anyone seen the flyers and called? Or did they even see the signs before they were taken down? There aren't many left up," said Elizabeth.

Teresa shrugged. "As I said, if the store suffers, my babies won't have a home. I must trust the fate of my fair felines to the hands of others."

"But ..." Elizabeth thought it must be hard for Teresa to be so bound by the store. If it was Tiger and Dolores, she'd be walking the streets until she found them. Elizabeth mentally renewed her pledge to do all she could.

"You'll want to begin these deliveries or you may not complete your appointed rounds before darkness halts your progress."

The bell attached to the door rang and Elizabeth looked up. It was Mr. Smith—again. Elizabeth thought he must be Read It Again's best customer. Then she looked at Teresa. The store owner had blushed a bright pink and was running her fingers through her orange curls.

"Mr. Smith! I'd forgotten …"

"Charles, you must call me Charles," Mr. Smith interrupted, patting Teresa's hand.

As Elizabeth watched the two of them, Teresa's face turned a deeper, brighter, almost *neon*, pink. Neither seemed to notice she was there. She cleared her throat. Their heads jerked, then turned toward her.

"If the books are ready to deliver," said Elizabeth.

"Yes, the books," Teresa said. She turned and ran into the edge of the display table.

"Are you okay?" Elizabeth asked.

Mr. Smith reached out for Teresa, but she was already limping toward the counter. "I'm fine," Teresa said, rubbing the spot on her thigh where she'd hit the table.

Teresa squatted, disappearing behind the counter, her hand appearing to set a bag on the counter. When the telephone rang, Teresa sprang up, hitting her head on the open cash register drawer.

Elizabeth and Mr. Smith rushed forward as Teresa sank to the floor, her hand pressed to the top of her head.

"Answer the telephone, please," Teresa said. She leaned against the wall, her eyes closed.

"Read It Again," Elizabeth said into the phone.

Mr. Smith leaned over Teresa, removing her hand and checking the knot already starting to form.

Elizabeth heard breathing on the end of the line, then a click followed by the dial tone. She hung up.

"Who was it?" Teresa asked.

"A hang-up," said Elizabeth.

All remaining traces of pink drained from Teresa's face, except for the red knot at the top of her forehead. "It was probably a wrong number," she said. Teresa stood slowly. "They said nothing?"

"Nothing," Elizabeth confirmed.

As Mr. Smith rose to stand beside Teresa, he brushed off the legs of his trousers. Elizabeth saw that orange-gold cat hair covered the lower part of his navy blue slacks.

"You have cats too?" asked Elizabeth.

"No, no pets," he said. "Must have picked it up here."

"My apologies," said Teresa. "I have a fabric brush you may borrow."

When Teresa stood beside Mr. Smith, Elizabeth noticed that her black skirt had no cat hair on it. Pretty odd considering she'd been sitting on the same floor where Mr. Smith had been kneeling. It looked to Elizabeth like a cat had rubbed against the man's legs, leaving the hair. And the only orange-gold cat in the store was missing.

"Your deliveries," said Teresa. She pushed three packages across to Elizabeth. "Two are destined for businesses in the immediate neighborhood, and this one will find a home with Mrs. Baker."

Elizabeth gathered the packages, stacking them in the order they would be delivered. She looked at the books scattered on the display table, then at Teresa.

"Gregory, will you join me for tea?" Teresa asked Mr. Smith.

"Charles," Mr. Smith said.

"Yes, of course, Charles," she corrected herself quickly.

"Let me know if you find out anything new about Finola and Duncan," Elizabeth said.

Mr. Smith brushed at the legs of his trousers again.

"Assuredly," said Teresa.

Reluctantly, Elizabeth turned toward the door. A man was standing at the curb, staring intently at the messy display table.

7

THE ELUSIVE GREGORY

"Teresa, look!" Elizabeth pointed.

Teresa took several steps toward the window. The man seemed to look directly at Teresa, who stopped when their eyes met. He stuck his hands in his jeans pockets and walked away.

The gesture seemed familiar to Elizabeth. Maybe it was something Justin did—no this man had done the same thing when he walked away from the bookstore that first day. It was Gregory! "Stop him!" cried Elizabeth.

Teresa looked at the pile of books on the table, took a few steps toward it, then looked back at the window. "He'll be back," she said. "And remember, if he was still employed by this establishment, you would not be here.

"If you truly want to be of assistance, deliver the packages. Then go home," said Teresa. "If you perchance see my cats on your journey, let me know. Otherwise, rein in your imagination and cease casting blame where none exists."

Teresa's words hit home. It wasn't the first time Elizabeth had been accused of having an overactive imagination. In fact, it was quickly becoming her theme song. "I'm sorry," Elizabeth said.

"I, too, am sorry," Teresa said. "I should not vent the negative feelings Gregory arouses in me upon you simply because you are near. I appreciate your stepping into the breach and aiding me when I needed your aid."

"I'd better go," Elizabeth said, still uncomfortable.

"Please, return tomorrow," said Teresa, walking with her to the door.

Elizabeth shrugged. As she walked away, she felt Teresa's eyes follow her all the way to the corner.

As soon as she turned the corner, Elizabeth stopped and leaned against the brick wall. She looked up and down the street, hoping to catch a glimpse of Gregory. He was nowhere in sight.

The packages were heavy. Elizabeth's arms already ached. At least the first two deliveries were close, and she would get rid of the heaviest books.

At the first store, a card shop, Elizabeth handed the books to the woman behind the counter. She was surprised when the woman gave her a dollar tip.

The second delivery was to a tiny office above a restaurant. The smell of hamburgers frying reminded her how close it was to supper-time.

She opened the door and stepped inside a small entryway. The door closed slowly behind her, cutting off the light and sound from the street. Elizabeth hurried up the steps. There was a note taped to the door of office number 1.

Please leave books at diner. Thanks. B. Wright

While she was reading the note, Elizabeth heard the door downstairs open. She waited to see if B. Wright had returned. "Hello?" Elizabeth looked over the railing and saw a figure standing in the shadows at the bottom of the stairs. "Mr. Wright?"

"Mr. Wrong," a man's voice answered. "Keep your nose out of business that doesn't concern you. Stay away from Read It Again. Teresa doesn't need your help."

Elizabeth broke out in a cold sweat. She was so frightened she couldn't move. She pulled away from the railing and searched frantically for a place to hide. What if the man came up the stairs after her? "Help me, Jesus," she whispered.

The door opened and slammed shut. Still pressed against the wall, Elizabeth waited to make sure the man didn't come up the stairs. Finally, she peeked over the railing again and saw that he was gone.

She flew down the steps, her footsteps echoing in the emptiness. At the bottom of the stairway there was a ball of paper. Elizabeth picked it up as she left the building.

Outside, she opened it. It was one of the flyers about Finola with a big X drawn across the cat's picture. Elizabeth let the paper drift to the ground. She thankfully stepped into the diner, full of lights and people. A young waitress with curly blonde hair piled on top of her head greeted Elizabeth.

"I have some books for B. Wright," Elizabeth said. Her voice sounded weak to her ears. She sat down at the counter on a red vinyl-covered stool.

"What happened to that cute Gregory who used to deliver the books?" the waitress asked, then added, "Not that you're not cute."

"Have you seem him lately?" Elizabeth asked.

"He usually stops in a couple times a week and sits over there in that corner, scribbling something in a notebook. Sometimes I see him look at me, then write. Kinda creepy, huh?"

"When was he here last?"

The waitress shrugged. "I used to tease him about what he was writing. Asked him if it was my phone number, you know? He's cute and smart. You have to be smart to write movies."

"You know what he's writing?" asked Elizabeth.

"Mystery movies," the girl whispered. "Murder mysteries."

Elizabeth shivered.

"He's going to make the movie himself if he has to. When you get back to the shop, tell him Lindy said hi." The waitress took the package of books and moved on to a new customer.

Gregory needed money? That might be a reason to take the cats, Elizabeth thought, if Teresa was willing to pay a cash reward. She got up off the stool and walked to the door, checking outside before she left the safety of the diner. Gregory was nowhere in sight.

Elizabeth was almost looking forward to her stop at Mrs. Baker's. At least she knew what to expect. At Mrs. Baker's door, Elizabeth squared her shoulders and smiled, then rang the doorbell. She listened to the woman's slow progress—the thump of the walker and the soft hiss of slippers across the floor. Locks turned and the door opened, safety chain still in place.

"It's Elizabeth Bryan, Mrs. Baker, with your books from Read It Again."

"More books?" Mrs. Baker asked.

"Yes, ma'am."

The chain dropped and the door opened a little wider than the first time Elizabeth had made a delivery. Elizabeth opened the storm door and passed the package to Mrs. Baker.

"Thank you," said the woman.

The kind tone surprised Elizabeth but not as much as the loud *meow* that came from inside the house.

"Mrs. Baker, is that a cat?" Elizabeth asked.

"No cats," Mrs. Baker said.

"I hear …"

"No cats." The door slammed in Elizabeth's face.

8

A HARD GUY TO FORGET

Elizabeth walked home deep in thought. For once she was glad to see Mr. Hamilton's car parked in front of the house. He'd said he knew Read It Again so maybe he knew Gregory. Elizabeth had a strong feeling that if she found Gregory, she'd find the cats—no matter what Teresa said. Hopefully, she'd find them before Finola's kittens were born.

And then there was the man who had followed her into the office building. Elizabeth was sure it was Gregory. Should she tell Mom? If she did, the job would definitely be over. She decided to try to find out a little more about Gregory first.

"I'm home," Elizabeth called out as she closed the front door.

"How was work?" Mom asked as Elizabeth joined her and Mr. Hamilton in the kitchen.

"Fine. I had to deliver another package to Mrs. Baker. And you know, I'm pretty sure I heard a cat meowing," said Elizabeth.

"Did those cats from the bookstore ever turn up?" Mr. Hamilton asked.

"Not yet," answered Elizabeth. "It's strange, though. The cats are missing from the bookstore and suddenly Mrs. Baker has a cat. But the noise couldn't have been a cat because the first time I made a delivery, Mrs. Baker threatened not to take the books if there was any cat hair on them."

"Having a pet to keep her company would be just what Mrs. Baker needs," said Mom. "But I think she rents that house, and pets may not be allowed."

Elizabeth thought that might explain why Mrs. Baker was so insistent that she didn't have a cat when Elizabeth knew she'd heard one.

"Speaking of which, your cat wants inside," said Mom.

Elizabeth walked over and opened the kitchen window to let Dolores into the house. As soon as the window opened, Tiger joined his sister on the ledge and pushed in first.

"You make her do all the work to get our

attention, then you come in first," Elizabeth said as the golden orange cat rubbed against her legs. Dolores paused on the window ledge, then jumped down and darted into the hall.

"Do you remember Gregory, the man who used to work at Read It Again?" Elizabeth asked Mr. Hamilton.

"He'd be a hard guy to forget."

"He's tall and skinny, with dark curly hair, really curly hair, right?" Elizabeth asked.

"That pretty much describes him," said Mr. Hamilton. "Why?"

"He's gone. He and Teresa had a big fight the first day I went to the store, and he walked out. I thought I saw him outside the shop tonight," said Elizabeth.

"It's his store. He has every right to be there," said Mr. Hamilton.

"What do you mean, 'It's his store'?"

"He and Teresa own it. They're brother and sister," Mr. Hamilton explained.

"You're kidding! Do you know where he lives?"

The phone rang before Mr. Hamilton could answer. Mom held the receiver out to Elizabeth. It was Amy Catherine.

"This weekend June Rae Wood, the woman who wrote *Man Who Loved Clowns*, is going to be autographing her books at Citybooks," Amy Catherine said, her voice high with excitement. "Mom said she'd drive us there if you'd like to go."

"What time?" Elizabeth asked. She had a job now and might have to work.

"At three in the afternoon. Afterward we could get some pizza or something, if you want," Amy Catherine said.

"Let me ask Teresa if I have to work, and if I don't, I'd like to go," said Elizabeth. This would be her first chance to meet a real author. Mrs. Wood had visited her school in the spring, but she'd talked to the entire seventh grade as a group. There hadn't been a chance to ask questions. Besides, Elizabeth hadn't read the book then. If she got a few more tips, she might have enough money to buy a copy and have the author autograph it.

"Call me and let me know if you can go," said Amy Catherine.

"Thanks for asking me," said Elizabeth. She hung up. "Amy Catherine invited me to go to an autographing Saturday. June Rae Wood."

"How exciting!" said Mom. "I wish I could go."

"That's when we're going to paper Mike's room," said Mr. Hamilton.

"I know," said Mom, making a face.

Elizabeth decided she'd definitely be somewhere other than home on Saturday.

"I'm hungry," said Mike, joining them in the kitchen.

"Set the table, and it'll be ready in a minute," said Mom.

"So do you know where Gregory lives?" Elizabeth asked again.

"I thought he lived upstairs over the shop," said Mr. Hamilton.

"He doesn't live there now. Teresa does," said Elizabeth.

"Teresa lived there too, but she was gone so much taking that big cat to shows …"

"You knew Finola was a champion cat?"

"I knew she went to lots of cat shows. But she retired last year, I think," said Mr. Hamilton.

"And Gregory?"

"He wants to be a writer. He's always scribbling away in notebooks. One time he told me he was writing about the murder that took place at the store."

"There really was a murder there?" Elizabeth asked.

"A robbery, they think. The guy shot the owner, but they never caught him. I think it was a drug store then," said Mr. Hamilton. "Gregory's been doing research for years trying to find out who did it. One of my friends in the police department says he's a real pest."

The phone rang again. Elizabeth answered, hoping it was Justin. She wanted to fill him in on the latest. But it was Meghan.

"I got two tickets to go see *Cinderella* at Stages Theater on Saturday afternoon. Remember how we said we wanted to go? Someone gave them to Mom, and she said we could use them. She'll even take us, and since it's the matinee, we can go out and eat afterward."

Elizabeth didn't say anything for a minute. Meghan sounded so excited, and it would be fun to go.

"Are you there? Are you asking your mom?" Meghan asked, her voice changing.

"I'd really like to go, but I can't," said Elizabeth. For a moment she considered saying that they were wallpapering, and she'd promised to help, but if Mom heard her lie, wallpapering is exactly what Elizabeth would be doing all weekend.

Elizabeth took a deep breath. "Amy Catherine just called and invited me to go someplace with her on Saturday afternoon."

The silence moved to Meghan's end of the telephone line. Then she spoke stiffly. "I've been putting up with Justin all year, always butting in when we're trying to do something, and I've finally decided he's all right. But is Amy Catherine always going to be around too? Elizabeth, I don't think you want a friend. You want a gang." Before Elizabeth could say anything, Meghan hung up.

"Dinner's ready," said Mom.

"Let me call Meghan back really fast," said Elizabeth, starting to dial.

Mom pushed down the receiver hook. "We all sit down, say grace, and eat together. You can talk to Meghan *after* dinner."

But will Meghan talk to *me*, Elizabeth worried. Help me know how to be her friend, God, she prayed.

2

A New Message

"After you left, Teresa was rushing to get me out of the store when Mr. Smith showed up," Elizabeth explained to Justin after school the next day. "He had hair all over his pants like a cat had been rubbing against him, but he said he didn't have a cat."

"So you think the hair on Mr. Smith's pants means he has Teresa's cats?" asked Justin.

"I don't really think that. Mr. Smith and Teresa *like* one another. You know, boyfriend-and-girlfriend like one another," said Elizabeth.

"What's weird about that?" Justin asked with a grin.

Elizabeth ignored him and thought for a moment. "Where did he get the cat hair?"

"Why would he take the cats if he *likes* her?" Justin asked.

"Shhh!" said Elizabeth. She was trying to think.

"Why?" Justin asked again.

"He finds the cats and brings them home and Teresa thinks he's a hero," Elizabeth answered.

"I don't know. That's a lot of work."

"Then there's Gregory, Teresa's brother."

"Her brother? I thought he just worked for her," said Justin.

"Mr. Hamilton said they own the store together and even lived together upstairs. You know, I think I saw Gregory outside the shop, staring in the window yesterday.

"Then when I went into an office building to deliver books, someone followed me. I couldn't see clearly, but I'm pretty sure it was the same man who was in front of the store. He told me to stay away from Read It Again and Teresa." Just the thought brought back the fear Elizabeth had felt.

"And the waitress in the diner below the office told me that Gregory wants to make a movie about that murder at the store, so he probably needs money," Elizabeth added.

"You told your mom about this, didn't you? or the police?" Justin asked. He put his arm around Elizabeth.

"I couldn't. Mom would make me quit the job. Besides I think it was Gregory."

"You know what Gregory looks like?" asked Justin.

"He almost knocked me down that first day. How could I forget him? I couldn't see the person who was at the bottom of the stairs. But I just know it had to be him."

"I don't like that at all," said Justin.

"If we knew where Gregory was now, we could check and make sure he doesn't have Finola and Duncan," said Elizabeth.

"How?"

"Knock on the door and listen for a cat." That reminded Elizabeth of the incident at Mrs. Baker's. "Remember how Mrs. Baker made a big deal out of cat hair the first time we delivered books to her?"

Justin shrugged and nodded.

"Yesterday I delivered books to her again, and I know I heard a cat in her house. She said there wasn't a cat, of course."

"You think Mrs. Baker catnapped Finola? She can barely walk."

"I don't *think* she did," said Elizabeth, "but

it's something to keep in mind."

"I'd say don't bother," said Justin. "Hey, how come Meghan isn't here putting her two cents in on this?" They were almost at the store.

Elizabeth felt a stab at the mention of Meghan's name. Her best friend had barely spoken to her all day, except to make excuses about why she couldn't talk. Elizabeth needed to tell Meghan why she hadn't called her back last night. Meghan knew Mom's rule about homework first and telephone second, but Meghan didn't know that her homework had kept her busy until after nine—too late for a phone call, Mom had said.

"She had something else to do," said Elizabeth, not ready to explain everything to Justin. She'd see Meghan at dance class tonight and try to talk to her.

"Do you have any ideas on how to find Gregory?" Elizabeth asked.

"My first plan of action would be to look in the phone book," said Justin. "Or wait until he finds you again."

"Stop saying that," said Elizabeth. "Even if he's got a new place to live, he wouldn't be in the phone book yet. Besides, I don't even know his last name."

"Same as Teresa's," said Justin.

"I don't know hers either. Remember I asked her and she said to call her Teresa."

"Ask her again," said Justin. "Then call directory assistance and see if there's a new listing for Gregory."

"Maybe," said Elizabeth, deciding to wait and see what kind of mood Teresa was in.

As they walked by the display window, Elizabeth checked the table. She stopped. "Look. I told you."

Five books were all standing upright and read, title by title, *Deep, Dark Friday Night, When the Clock Strikes Ten, The Long Fingered Arm of the Hollow Oak, Parkside.*

10

PUTTING THE PLAN INTO ACTION

"It's another message," Elizabeth whispered, then glanced furtively over her shoulder. "It's like a when and where."

"The when and where of what?" Justin asked in his regular voice.

"Shh!" Elizabeth put her finger to her lips. "A ransom maybe?"

"And Teresa put it out for anyone to see?" asked Justin, but in a lower voice.

"No one will get it except the catnapper—and us."

"It still doesn't tell us anything," said Justin.

Elizabeth noticed he was looking at everyone passing by too. "Friday night at 10 P.M. in a hollow oak at parkside," she stated.

"Parkside?" Justin asked. "Where is that exactly?"

"I don't know," said Elizabeth, "yet."

"And what are you going to do about it anyway?" Justin asked.

"If we find out where Gregory lives and find out he has the cats, we won't have to do anything. We can tell Teresa or the police," said Elizabeth.

"Then that is your mission, should you choose to accept it," said Justin. "I have newspapers to deliver."

"See you tomorrow. We can go to Gregory's after school," said Elizabeth.

"*If* you find out where he lives."

"Piece of cake," said Elizabeth with a confidence she didn't entirely feel.

Teresa looked up from a computer printout spread on the counter when Elizabeth entered the shop. Teresa had a dark blue and purple bruise with flecks of yellow through it where she'd hit her head the day before. The bruise almost perfectly matched the dark circles under Teresa's eyes.

"Are you okay?" Elizabeth asked.

Teresa nodded. "A little fatigued perhaps."

"Do you have any books for me to deliver?"

Elizabeth asked.

"Not today," Teresa answered with an attempt at a smile.

Elizabeth heard loud meows from the apartment upstairs. "Is Finola back?"

"That's Shelley and Keats," said Teresa. "Both are extremely displeased with my decision to imprison them in the tower. However, it is their safety I have at heart."

"Can I help you do anything else?" Elizabeth wandered over to the display table in front of the window and reached for the first book.

"No!" Teresa said sharply, then added in a softer tone. "I mean, not at the present. Perhaps we should arrange a stay of our business arrangement. I will contact you when I need your assistance. Until then, you must go your merry way."

Elizabeth moved to the counter, making sure she left the books in exactly the same order they'd been in before she touched them. "You mean you don't want me hanging around?"

"I'm certain a young girl has more exciting things to do than keep company in a boring used-book store," Teresa said.

"I could fix up some displays for you. That table is in a perfect spot. We could do mysteries."

"No, no. Those books are fine where they are. They're new. I like to display new books," Teresa said.

Elizabeth traced circles in the wood of the counter. "What's your last name?"

"Smythe," Teresa said, but she had a puzzled look on her face.

"Like Smith only with a *y*?"

"And an *e* on the end," said Teresa, "not at all like Smith."

Elizabeth thought about Mr. Smith and Miss Smythe. If they married, how would they spell it? Or would Teresa become Mrs. Smythe-Smith? "Is Mr. Smith coming in today?" she asked.

Teresa blushed. "He may drop by for a spot of tea."

"Do you have any idea when Gregory might be back?" Elizabeth asked.

"No," Teresa said, "and if I knew …"

Elizabeth waited for her to finish.

"You should run along now and pursue your academic interests, or play with some of your friends, or whatever," Teresa said, returning to her printout.

"You'll call me? soon?" asked Elizabeth.

"When I have something. Bye now," said Teresa, not bothering to walk Elizabeth to the door this time.

Elizabeth found a note from her mother when she got home.

Took Mike to Cub Scouts. Be home to drive you to dance class. Sandwich in the fridge. Drink milk.   *Love, Mom*

Elizabeth decided this would be a good time to try to find Gregory. She found the phone book and dialed the directory assistance number. She asked for a Gregory Smythe. She spelled the last name. There were no listings.

"What about a G. Smythe?" she asked.

"One moment," the operator said.

A recording gave her two phone numbers, one for a G. S. Smythe and the other for a G. W. She punched in G. S.'s number.

An answering machine picked up after the second ring. A young child's voice said, "My mommy and daddy can't come to the phone right now because they're paying attention to me. They'll call you back as soon as I leave for college." Elizabeth figured that wasn't Gregory.

An elderly woman answered at the next number. "May I speak to Gregory, please?" Elizabeth asked.

"Gregory? Gregory who?" the woman asked.

"Gregory Smythe," said Elizabeth.

"Who is this?" asked the woman.

"I'm trying to locate Gregory Smythe."

"My husband passed on several years ago, young lady, and we never bought any of that siding you're always trying to sell anyway. Our house is brick." She hung up.

Elizabeth decided she'd have to go with Plan B to find Gregory and the catnapped cats— as soon as she came up with a Plan B.

11

MAKING UP
WITH MEGHAN

Meghan was already stretching when Elizabeth arrived at dance class. Elizabeth changed into tap shoes and joined her.

"I've been looking for you all day," said Elizabeth.

Meghan leaned forward and touched her head to her knees. She didn't say a word.

"I'm almost sure that Gregory, the guy who used to work at Read It Again—he's Teresa's brother, by the way—has the cats."

Meghan turned her face toward Elizabeth but continued to silently stretch.

"He followed me when I was delivering books for Teresa and told me to stay away from the bookstore. Now Teresa says she doesn't need me."

"Elizabeth, Meghan, are you here to dance

or talk?" Miss Karen, their teacher, interrupted.

The girls joined the class in the center of the studio.

"I'll tell you the rest after," Elizabeth managed to whisper.

Meghan nodded and even smiled a shadow of her normal smile, giving Elizabeth hope that her friend was not as mad as she had been.

By the end of the tap class, Elizabeth was sweating. She dropped to the floor beside her dance bag and toweled off her face and neck.

Meghan hobbled over and sat beside Elizabeth. "First that ballet clinic and now this. I'm too old." She stretched out on the floor.

"You sound like our moms at the end of one of our classes. But you're not allowed to quit!" Elizabeth said, fanning Meghan with a towel. Elizabeth and Meghan had started the tap class with their moms, but both women had dropped the class after the summer.

Elizabeth laughed and dropped the towel over Meghan's face. "Move closer and talk loud so I'll be sure to hear you," said Meghan.

"I think Teresa is using books in the window to leave Gregory messages. That's why she didn't want you to block it the other day. I tried to find Gregory by calling directory assistance. I thought maybe he'd have gotten a phone, but it didn't work. The only other plan of action I came up with is to follow Teresa when she drops off the money, then follow whoever picks it up and rescue the cats. I'm almost sure it's Gregory, but it could be Mr. Smith. He comes in the store all the time. It could even be Mrs. Baker."

"Wait a minute, you want to follow someone who threatened you?"

"He didn't really threaten me," said Elizabeth.

"And if Gregory didn't take the cats, you think Mrs. Baker might have taken them? You're talking about the same Mrs. Baker who goes to our church, right? Get real."

"She has a cat at her house, and she didn't until Finola and Duncan disappeared," said Elizabeth.

"Why don't we, I mean *you*, just go wherever the message says to go?"

"Because I don't know exactly where the message says to go," said Elizabeth.

"What's the message?" Meghan asked.

"Something about Friday at ten and a hollow oak tree at parkside. I think it means that she'll leave the money in a tree someplace on Friday at 10 P.M. That's *tomorrow*."

"Parkside?" asked Meghan.

"That's the part I don't understand. How many parks are there around here?" asked Elizabeth.

"Unless it's Parkside, you know, the street that runs alongside that little park by Field School," said Meghan.

"There's a street with that name?"

Meghan sat up. "We used to go to that park when I was little. Sometimes I take my cousins there when I'm baby-sitting. Parkside isn't really a street, more like a path big enough for cars. I think they use it to go in and pick up trash."

Elizabeth's mind raced. Now she knew when and where the ransom would be picked up—thanks to Meghan. The only thing she didn't know for sure was *who* would be there to collect it.

"I've really missed you this week," Elizabeth said. She didn't speak very loudly, and she didn't look at Meghan, afraid of her reaction.

"I've missed you too," said Meghan.

"I could have a hundred other friends, a gang even, and none of them would be like you.

Think you could spend the night tomorrow night?" Elizabeth asked.

"I'll ask," said Meghan. She stuffed her tap shoes in her dance bag, then stood up. Elizabeth stood too. "My mom's probably here," said Meghan.

"Call me and let me know about tomorrow night," Elizabeth said.

The girls looked at one another. Meghan reached out at the same moment Elizabeth did, and they gave one another a quick hug. Thanks, God, Elizabeth thought and smiled at her best friend.

12

WHEN
THE CLOCK
STRIKES 10

Elizabeth kept close to the wall, dodging kids who were grabbing hats and backpacks and knocking books to the floor. It seemed even noisier than usual for a Friday afternoon. When she finally made it to Justin's locker, he was ready to go. A Koosh ball came flying toward them, and Justin caught it with his free hand, then tossed it back to Rich.

"I start my paper route today," Rich yelled.

"I'll see you there," Justin said.

"I have to wait for Meghan," said Elizabeth. "She's spending the night with me."

"What are you going to do?" Justin asked.

"That's what I wanted to talk to you about," said Elizabeth. "Meghan knows what … er …

where Parkside is."

"Parkside?" Justin looked like he'd never heard the word before.

"As in the message Teresa left for the cat-napper—Friday at 10, hollow oak, parkside," Elizabeth explained.

"And?"

"I want to know who took Finola and Duncan, and I want to get them back for Teresa," said Elizabeth.

"Seems like Teresa has it under control, although I still don't understand why she doesn't go to the police," said Justin.

Meghan ran up to them, her backpack hanging on her shoulder by one strap. "Sorry I'm late," she said breathlessly.

"I was telling Justin about Parkside," said Elizabeth.

"Is he going?" asked Meghan.

"Wait a minute, going where?" Justin took a step away from Elizabeth.

"We could go and watch to see who picks up the money and then make sure the cats get back to Teresa safely," said Elizabeth.

"Maybe we should tell the police what's going on," said Justin.

"No way!" Elizabeth and Meghan said together.

"Teresa might never get the cats back if the catnapper sees the police," said Elizabeth.

"They probably know how to handle these things so the catnapper doesn't know they're there," Justin said.

"We'll just watch, you know, sort of a back-up for Teresa," said Elizabeth. "You'll be sorry if you miss this. And anyway, she shouldn't have to pay to get her own cats back, especially pay her own brother. We can tell the police when the cats are safe. We'll be witnesses." Goose bumps rippled down Elizabeth's arms and legs as she imagined the evening's adventure.

"Your mom is going to let you go wandering around at 10 o'clock at night?" asked Justin in disbelief.

"Not exactly," said Elizabeth. She looked quickly at Meghan, then back at Justin.

"Uh-oh," he said.

"We thought if we told Mom we were watching videos at your house, it would be okay. We can call her about nine-thirty and say we got started late and the movie won't be over until eleven or so. That should give us plenty of time," said Elizabeth.

"And what am I supposed to tell my mom?"

"That you're going to be watching videos at my house," Elizabeth said with a somewhat guilty expression.

"It's only a *little* fib," said Meghan. "And it's to help somebody."

"You probably need me to make sure you don't get in any trouble," said Justin.

"No we don't!" Meghan and Elizabeth shouted. Justin laughed.

"Meet us at the video store at 7 P.M. ," said Elizabeth. "We can actually go to your house and watch a movie, if your mom's not home. Or we can get some pizza or something."

"Pizza! Yummy," said Meghan.

"See you at seven," agreed Justin.

Mr. Hamilton dropped Meghan and Elizabeth off at the video store promptly at seven.

"Tell Mom I'll call and let her know what time to pick us up," said Elizabeth. Her heart did a flip as she realized how easily her plan was working. She'd never lied so blatantly to her mom before. But wasn't it for a good cause?

"You have a good time," said Mr. Hamilton. "Sure you don't want me to wait and drive you to Justin's?"

"We might stop and get some pizza on the way," said Meghan.

"We just finished eating," Mr. Hamilton said.

"Dessert," responded Meghan with a laugh.

Elizabeth slammed the car door and waved as Mr. Hamilton drove away.

Justin was already waiting inside the video store. "I have my mom's video card," he said, "just in case you want to rent anything."

"It should be something we've already seen, in case Mom asks," said Elizabeth.

"*Star Wars?*" suggested Justin. Elizabeth wrinkled her nose.

"*Beauty and the Beast?*" asked Meghan. Justin shook his head.

"*Little Women?*" Elizabeth suggested.

"No," said Meghan. "We've seen it five times already." Justin agreed.

"A video would be just one more thing to carry," said Elizabeth.

"Then let's just go for pizza," said Meghan. On the way to Pizza Royale, they passed

Read It Again. The store was dark. Only a red exit light gleamed in the back of the store.

Elizabeth pressed her face against the window and looked at the table. The same books were still lined up like silent soldiers awaiting their next command. Taking a step backward, she looked at the windows above the shop—all dark.

"Do you think Teresa is already on her way to the park?" Elizabeth asked anxiously.

"She's probably eating dinner or at a movie. Maybe she's with that Mr. Smith you said comes in all the time," said Meghan.

"I don't want to miss anything," said Elizabeth.

"We won't," said Justin. "C'mon."

Elizabeth let Meghan and Justin order while she found a booth at the back of the restaurant. Justin and Meghan ate while Elizabeth nibbled at the pizza.

Elizabeth watched the clock. The hands seemed to move slower and slower as the time to leave for the park grew near. She tried to pay attention to the conversation, but she didn't say much. When they finished the pizza, Justin challenged Meghan and Elizabeth to a game of Daytona USA in the video arcade.

Elizabeth tagged along and watched as Meghan trounced Justin. He barely had time to see the cars coming. "Where'd you learn to play like that?" he asked.

"Practice," said Meghan.

"I could have told you that you didn't stand a chance," said Elizabeth.

"But you didn't!" Justin cried out.

The girls laughed.

"Wait till next time," said Justin.

"Any time," said Meghan.

"I think Elizabeth is ready to go," Justin whispered to Meghan.

"What gave you that idea? Because she has her jacket on? Because she keeps watching the clock? Because she keeps looking at the door?" Meghan asked.

"C'mon, you guys. I'm trying to be patient," Elizabeth said. "It's nine-thirty. Let me call my mom real quick." She went to a pay phone and dialed home. The answering machine picked up.

"It's me, Elizabeth," she said. "We got kind of a late start on the movie, so I'll call you when it's over. Justin said he'd walk us home. Talk to you later. Bye!"

"Okay?" said Meghan.

"No one was home." Elizabeth felt a little nervous about that. She hoped Mom wouldn't stop by Justin's house on the way home from wherever she was. She'd freak if she found out they weren't there and hadn't been all evening.

"Do you know the park I'm talking about?" Meghan asked. "It isn't far from here, but it's in the opposite direction from your house."

"I think I know," said Elizabeth.

Meghan led them through the business district along a well-lighted main street. About four blocks from downtown, they turned on to a side street. The lights were a little farther apart.

"We lived in this neighborhood when I was little," said Meghan.

The school appeared in an island of bright lights. "The park is on the other side of the school. There's a woods behind the park and some houses on the other side of the woods," Meghan explained.

Elizabeth's eyes moved constantly, watching for Teresa or the catnapper. The three of them seemed to be the only ones out. Only one car had passed them since they'd turned off the main street. The park was small—three swings, a sandbox, a picnic table, and a paved area with a basketball hoop. One lonely light burned near the basketball hoop.

Meghan led them through the open ground to a narrow gravel road.

"That must be the tree," said Elizabeth. One large tree stood alone in the far corner of the park right next to the road.

"What now?" asked Justin.

Across the gravel road, Elizabeth saw a thicket of bushes. "We can go over there and watch from behind all those bushes," she said.

"Can't we sit on the swings?" said Meghan. "No telling what else is in there."

"We'll scare him off if he sees us," said Elizabeth.

"How do you know it's a him?" asked Justin. "It could be Mrs. Baker."

They'd all been talking in hushed voices, but when Justin mentioned Mrs. Baker, Meghan hooted in laughter, then clapped her hand over her mouth to muffle it.

"Quiet! I definitely heard a cat at her house," said Elizabeth.

"Mrs. Baker can barely walk," whispered Meghan.

Elizabeth hushed her and led the way to the bushes. Their footsteps on the gravel sounded unusually loud to her.

"I can't see anything," said Meghan as she carefully cleared herself an island in the midst of the brush.

"You guys stay here a minute. I'll be right back." Elizabeth ran along the bushes, looked for any sign of people approaching, then darted to the tree. She saw it immediately—a Read It Again bag was stuffed in the lowest V of the tree. She returned to her friends, keeping her eyes on the bag.

"What time is it?" Elizabeth asked.

"Five to ten," answered Justin.

They all heard it at the same time and froze statue still as footsteps crunched along the gravel road. Elizabeth peeked through the tiny window she'd cleared in the bushes and saw jeans, a denim jacket, and dark curly hair—Gregory. But there was no sign of the cats.

13

THE DELIVERY

Gregory approached the tree, paused, and looked around. To Elizabeth, it seemed like he was looking straight into their hiding place. His body blocked her view of the tree, but Elizabeth saw the plastic bag drift to the ground as Gregory stuck his hands in his pockets. He looked around again and headed straight toward them.

Elizabeth held her breath until he passed by. He cut through the middle of the park to the sidewalk and turned toward the main street.

"He didn't bring the cats," said Justin.

"Now that we have him, I'm not going to let him out of my sight until I know those cats are safe. C'mon." Elizabeth ran through the park, slowing as she approached the street. Gregory was walking fast. She followed.

Justin pulled on her jacket and Elizabeth jerked loose. "Where do you think you're going?" he asked.

"I want to know where he's going," said Elizabeth. "He still has the cats."

"Maybe he already left them at the shop," suggested Meghan.

"I don't want to lose him," said Elizabeth. She couldn't be sure, but it sounded like Gregory was *whistling*.

Always staying about a block behind, they followed Gregory to the main street. Elizabeth relaxed a little when he turned onto the brightly lit road. Here they could blend in with other people walking along.

He passed through the business district and into a familiar residential neighborhood. Elizabeth was only a little surprised when he walked up to Mrs. Baker's house. Gregory took out a key and unlocked the front door.

"I did hear a cat," Elizabeth said. "I wonder if Gregory was there when I delivered the books?"

"What now?" asked Meghan.

"Let's wait a minute." They moved off the sidewalk into the shadow of a large tree in the neighbor's yard. The front door opened and light spilled out onto the porch. Duncan, the orange striped cat, stepped out of the house followed by Gregory. The cat wrapped himself around the man's legs, almost tripping him.

Gregory reached into the house and brought out a suitcase, then a backpack. He cut across the lawn to the driveway and disappeared along the side of the house. Duncan followed him.

A car started, then died, then started again. Exhaust preceded an ancient black car into the street.

"He's taking them back now," said Justin.

Elizabeth put her hand on his arm, keeping him out of sight until she was sure the car was gone. "But where's Finola?" she asked.

Just then Duncan reappeared from around the side of the house, meowing loudly. He jumped onto the porch and clawed at the screen door.

"He left the door to Mrs. Baker's house wide open!" Elizabeth said. She crossed the yard to the porch, holding out her hand and calling, "Kitty, kitty."

Duncan turned and came straight to Elizabeth, sniffed her hand, then sprawled on the sidewalk at her feet and flopped back and forth until she leaned down and petted him. He jumped up and ran back to the door, meowing again. He took a few steps toward Elizabeth, then ran back to the door. Justin and Meghan hadn't moved from the shadows at the edge of the yard.

Elizabeth climbed the steps to the porch and peered through the storm door. "Mrs. Baker?" she called. Mrs. Baker appeared at the far end of a dimly lit hallway. "It's Elizabeth Bryan," Elizabeth called out.

"Delivering books at this hour?" Mrs. Baker asked.

"Not tonight. There's a cat out here trying to get in your house, Mrs. Baker," Elizabeth said.

"It's not my cat. He belongs to Gregory. Gregory's gone to get help for the other cat. She's going to have kittens we think," said Mrs. Baker, looking over her shoulder.

Elizabeth thought about the suitcase Gregory had put in the car and the backpack. She didn't think he'd packed to go to the vet. Justin and Meghan had moved to the sidewalk.

"The poor little cat is having a hard time of it," said Mrs. Baker, her voice wavering.

"Do you think I could help?" Elizabeth

asked. She didn't want anything to happen to Finola now that they'd located her.

"Maybe you could. I don't know much about animals. She doesn't seem to be in pain, just tired, and she's been trying to birth the kittens for an awfully long time."

"Finola is having her kittens," Elizabeth said to Justin and Meghan. They followed her into the house.

At the door to the kitchen, everyone stopped. Finola was on her side in a shallow box, panting heavily. She strained, then laid her head down and closed her eyes.

Elizabeth moved a little closer. She thought she saw something when Finola strained again. She watched in wonder as a tiny perfect kitten emerged. Finola busied herself licking the newborn kitten, then resumed panting.

Elizabeth turned to her friends. Their eyes were glued on Finola, wide with wonder. Finola continued to strain, but Elizabeth couldn't see any sign of another kitten. After awhile, the mother cat laid her head down and closed her eyes.

Fear gripped Elizabeth. She moved a little closer to try to see if there was a problem. The grip tightened when Elizabeth saw a kitten's tiny feet. She was sure the first kitten had been born head first.

"Somebody call my mom," Elizabeth said. "Finola needs help, and I don't know what to do."

"Gregory is getting us help," said Mrs. Baker. "He should be back any minute."

"Gregory took his suitcase with him when he left, Mrs. Baker. I don't want to count on him showing up anytime soon," said Elizabeth as kindly as she could.

"Suitcase? But he borrowed my car," said Mrs. Baker.

"Don't worry about that now," said Elizabeth. "Tell Mom to hurry, Meghan." She sat cross-legged near Finola and waited.

Please, God, let her be all right, Elizabeth prayed. Why, oh, why, didn't I tell Teresa when I first thought the cats were with Mrs. Baker? Elizabeth asked herself.

It seemed like forever before Meghan came to say that Elizabeth's mom and Mr. Hamilton were on the way. Elizabeth wanted to pet Finola, comfort her, but she was afraid she'd scare the cat. Finola rested more and more often, and her panting seemed weaker and weaker.

A car pulled into the driveway. "It's them," Meghan called from her post at the front door.

Elizabeth jumped up. "The kitten is coming out the wrong way," she said as Mom and Mr. Hamilton came into the kitchen. "And Finola is getting tired."

"See if you can find her a little milk or some food," Mr. Hamilton said. He checked the mother cat while Elizabeth checked the refrigerator. She found an open quart of milk and poured what was left of it into a bowl she found on the floor. Mr. Hamilton washed his hands, then let Finola lap at the milk.

"I don't know what's keeping Gregory," Mrs. Baker said.

Elizabeth's mother led the woman into the living room. Elizabeth followed them. Justin was sitting on the sofa holding Duncan, who was purring loudly.

Mom gave Elizabeth a hug. "I can't imagine what is going on here," she said, "but you can tell me later."

Elizabeth took a deep breath as she realized the explaining she would have to do, but allowed herself to relax in her mother's arms for a moment.

"The kitten is fine," Mr. Hamilton called out.

Elizabeth peeked in to see Finola licking a second baby. "Do you think that's all?" Elizabeth asked. Mr. Hamilton shook his head.

"Will you call Teresa at Read It Again?" Elizabeth asked her mom. "These are her cats."

"Gregory doesn't want to see his sister," said Mrs. Baker. "And the cats belong to him no matter what that woman says."

"Here comes another one," Mr. Hamilton said. Justin and Meghan stood behind Elizabeth. Elizabeth was struck again by the miracle of new life.

"It's like God is right here with us," Justin whispered.

"It's fantastic," said Meghan.

Thanks, God, Elizabeth prayed, and for the first time, her prayer of thanks included Mr. Hamilton.

14
UNEXPECTED (AND EXPECTED) ANSWERS

"I thought you didn't like cats," Elizabeth said to Mr. Hamilton.

Teresa and Mr. Smith had shown up at Mrs. Baker's in record time. When Gregory still hadn't shown up, Mrs. Baker decided it was all right for Teresa to take charge of the new mother and babies.

"I never said I didn't like cats," Mr. Hamilton said. "I grew up on a farm and they were always there—along with all the other rodents." He reached out and ruffled Elizabeth's hair.

"You were amazing with Finola. I thought she was going to die—and the kittens too," Elizabeth confessed.

"All in a day's work," Mr. Hamilton said.

"How can I ever thank you for returning my Finola and Duncan to me safe and sound?" Teresa asked, joining them.

"I'm glad they're okay. All I could think about was how I'd feel if it was Tiger or Dolores who was missing," said Elizabeth. "Well, and how mad I was at the person who took them."

"I don't think Gregory will get very far," said Mom. "Mrs. Baker's car is rather noticeable, and the police also have the license number."

"Such a nice young man. Reminded me of my Stephen," Mrs. Baker said. "And it was so nice to have a young person in the house again." She dabbed at her eyes with a tissue.

Teresa's eyes were also wet. She sat beside Mrs. Baker and put her arms around the old woman. "I would have given Gregory the money if he'd only asked. It wasn't necessary for him to abduct my babies."

She looked at Elizabeth. "And I couldn't call the police on my own brother. I thought he'd come to his senses eventually. Gregory has always liked to play games. That's why I sent the message in the book titles. He liked things like that. You were so clever to figure out our code!"

Teresa choked back a sob. "When the clock struck eleven and my cats were still missing, I must admit I began to doubt my trust in my brother. He said as soon as he saw the green of my money, the cats would be returned."

Mr. Smith put his hand on Teresa's shoulder and gave her a comforting smile.

Elizabeth wasn't sure she could be as forgiving as Teresa. Jesus said to forgive people who hurt you. He even forgave the people who nailed Him to the cross. Maybe He was helping Teresa to forgive.

"You have some explaining to do, young lady," Mom said, "I expected you to be at Justin's house. And by now, you all should be home in bed. Aunt Nan is going to think we've abandoned Mike."

"You must accept one of Finola's offspring in appreciation for all you've done," Teresa said to Elizabeth.

Elizabeth looked at Mom. She wanted one of the kittens. She felt a special bond with them.

"We already have two cats," Mom said.

Mr. Hamilton cleared his throat. "Maybe I'll take one, the little backward gray one," he said.

Elizabeth was almost as surprised by the

rush of warmth she felt for Mr. Hamilton as she was by his words.

"Is there one for me?" Mrs. Baker asked. "I've so enjoyed watching the two big ones play the last few days. And my allergies haven't acted up at all. You must keep your cats very clean. But I am a little worried about taking care of a baby."

"I have just the cat for you," said Mr. Smith. "I was worried about Teresa, she missed her cats so much. I went to the Humane Society and picked out a beautiful gold tiger stripe to give to her. But now I don't know if she needs another cat."

Teresa kissed the elf-man on the cheek. "I'd much rather Mrs. Baker had the cat."

"I'll bring it by tomorrow," said Mr. Smith.

"Mrs. Baker has graciously agreed that Finola and I can stay the night with her. It will give Finola a chance to rest and regain her strength before we move her back home," said Teresa.

"Elizabeth, I insist you accept the book you've been toiling so diligently to earn," Teresa said. "And each of you must visit me at Read It Again and choose an appropriate reward from the shelves. It's the least I can do."

"But I *like* working for you," Elizabeth said.

"You may continue to do so, if you desire," said Teresa. "I have two deliveries tomorrow."

"Tell everyone good night," Mom said. "We can talk about the job later."

Teresa, and then Mr. Smith, shook hands with everyone and made each promise to come to Read It Again for a proper thank-you.

The ride home was quiet. They dropped Justin at his house, then Mr. Hamilton drove to Elizabeth's house.

"Good night," Elizabeth said as she got out of the car. "And Don …"

Mr. Hamilton looked at her, surprise quickly turning to pleasure as a smile spread over his face.

"Thanks again for saving Finola."

"My pleasure."

Mom put her arm around Elizabeth as they walked to the house, trailing Meghan.

"I know what you mean now when you say God works in mysterious ways," Elizabeth said.

"Yes?" said Mom.

"I think He answered two of my prayers tonight," said Elizabeth. "One the way I wanted it to turn out and the other—well, that one surprised me."

"I think He's answered mine too," said Mom.

Elizabeth smiled. Aunt Nan always said if God's love was big enough to send His Son to die for the world, it was big enough to heal the hurt left behind when her dad died and went to live with Him in heaven. She and Mom turned and watched as Don drove out of sight.